FRED BOWEN

Ω
PEACHTREE
ATLANTA

Ω

Published by
PEACHTREE PUBLISHERS
1700 Chattahoochee Avenue
Atlanta, Georgia 30318-2112
www.peachtree-online.com

Printed and bound in April 2014 in the United States of America by
RR Donnelley & Sons in Harrisonburg, Virginia
10 9 8 7 6 5

Library of Congress Cataloging-in-Publication Data
    Bowen, Fred.
    Real hoops / by Fred Bowen.
        p. cm.
    Summary: When Ben and Logan go to a recreation center to practice bas-
ketball with more experienced players in hopes of getting on the freshman
team, they meet Hud, who could be the perfect point guard if he is willing to
listen to the coach.
    ISBN 978-1-56145-566-9 / 1-56145-566-0
    [1. Basketball—Fiction. 2. Coaching (Athletics)—Fiction. 3. Teamwork
(Sports)—Fiction. 4. Recreation centers—Fiction.] I. Title.
    PZ7.B6724Re 2011
    [Fic]—dc22
                                                2010030360

*For Bob Drummer, Carl Fink,
Jim Becker, and all the Court Jesters—
real basketball friends.*

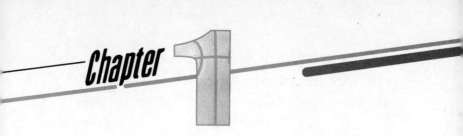

Chapter 1

Hey, Logan! I'm open!" Ben Williams shouted, raising his hand to call for the basketball.

Logan Moore was trapped. Two defenders were all over him, waving their arms wildly, trying to slap the ball from his hands. But Logan was tall and he held the ball high, out of their reach. When he heard Ben's voice, he turned and flicked him a two-handed pass.

Ben caught the ball and sent a jump shot spinning toward the hoop. The ball splashed through the chain net. A perfect swish!

"That's game," Ben said, walking over to the park's water fountain. "10–5."

"You want to play another?" Logan asked as he waited his turn for a drink. He stood with his head bent slightly forward, the way he always did around his shorter friends.

Ben looked around the park. He wiped his mouth with the back of his hand. "Nah, let's get out of here."

"Don't you want to play?" Logan said. "Tryouts for the freshman team are in a couple of weeks."

"I know," Ben said. "That's why I don't want to keep playing here. Nobody here can cover you...or me."

"So where do you want to go?"

"How about the Westwood Recreation Center?" Ben suggested.

"Westwood?"

"Yeah. They're supposed to have some really good games."

"A lot of older guys play over there," Logan said.

"That's why we should go," Ben said, running a hand through his sweaty hair. He was just a few inches shorter than Logan, but he looked every bit the athlete. "We aren't going to get any better playing against a bunch of little kids. The L7 bus goes right near the Center. Come on."

"You got money?"

"I've got enough for both of us."

Logan looked around at the other kids pushing up shots toward the basket. None of them were very good. "Okay. Let's go."

Minutes later, the two friends dropped onto the back seats of the L7 bus. Almost immediately they started talking about the upcoming basketball tryouts at Roosevelt High School. Ben and Logan had played together for years and they were both hopeful about making the freshman team.

"I figure we've got you at center," Ben said, confidently spinning the basketball in his hands. "And me at shooting guard."

"Andrew Milstein, Jordan Ferraro, and Alan Dawson can all play forward," Logan said.

"Yeah, and Sam Molina is big enough to back you up." Ben gazed out the bus window. The large green lawns of their neighborhood had given way to the tight, crowded streets of downtown. "We could use a point guard, though," Ben said. "We need somebody who can handle the ball, push it upcourt, and pass."

"Levon Efford is okay at point guard," Logan said, with a shrug.

"That's the problem," Ben said. "He's just *okay*."

"Eighth and Westwood," the driver announced.

"That's us," Ben said. The two boys scrambled off the bus and onto the sidewalk. They jogged toward the rec center, bounce-passing the basketball between them.

"There it is," Ben said. He pointed down the street to a large brick building surrounded by playing fields and a half-dozen outdoor basketball courts. The courts were filled with players and the sounds of balls hitting the pavement and clanging against loose metal rims.

"Looks just like our playground," Logan said, checking out the kids on the courts.

"The really good games are supposed to be inside," Ben said. He tucked the basketball under his arm and headed for the front doors.

A man with gray hair and reading glasses tilted on the end of his nose looked up from behind a long desk. "You boys new to Westwood?" he asked.

"Yeah," Ben said.

"Okay, then you'll have to sign in." The man nodded toward a nearby computer. "Just type your names."

"Do we have to pay?" Logan asked.

The man shook his head. "No, we just like to keep track of how many people use the Center." He looked at the ball under Ben's arm. "If you're looking for a good run, the best games are back there," he said. "And by the way, I'm Mr. Sims, the director."

"Thanks, Mr. Sims," Ben said. He and Logan walked past the desk and stood at the big Plexiglas window that overlooked the basketball court.

Just as the boys had expected, the games

were a mix of high school and college kids. Some of the players looked even older. There were two games going and a bunch of guys waiting in the bleachers. The games were fast and loud. Ben could hear the players' shouts through the glass.

"Who's got him?"

"Watch out for Hud!"

"Gimme the ball, gimme the ball!"

A skinny kid in baggy red shorts and a sweaty T-shirt dribbled downcourt at top speed. He cut right, bringing the defender with him. Then he flipped a no-look pass to his left. The pass flew straight into the hands of a player under the basket who quickly laid the ball against the backboard and into the net.

"Whoa! Nice pass," Logan said.

"I told you the games were better here," Ben said. "Let's go down."

The boys barreled through the door. As they scrambled down the steps, they saw the skinny kid in the red shorts drive to the basket and whip a wraparound pass to another player for another easy layup.

"That's game," the kid said as he turned to the sidelines. "Who's got next?"

Five players hustled onto the court to replace the losing team.

"Me and Ty got to go home," the player who scored the last basket called out.

The kid in the red shorts looked at Ben and Logan. "You guys want to run?"

"Sure," Ben said. "But what about those guys over there?"

The kid looked at the small clump of players talking to each other on the sidelines. "They're waiting for a game on another court," he said. "Come on."

"Okay." Ben smiled at Logan and the two of them jogged onto the court.

"I'm Hud," the kid said. "And we got Ice Man and Helicopter," he added, pointing at two older players. "Let's go."

The game was fast—much faster and rougher than the ones at Ben and Logan's regular playground. Players raced up and down the court, taking open jump shots. Ben hit his first three shots on passes from Hud.

"Hey, we got a shooter," Hud said with a grin.

But Hud was the player who controlled the action. His passes were amazing. He always got the ball to teammates who could make open jumpers and easy layups. After about an hour of nonstop hoops and several wins, Ben, Logan, and Hud took a break in the wooden stands.

"You guys can really play," Hud said to Ben and Logan. "What team are you on?"

"Well, we have to try out first. But we're going to play for the Roosevelt freshman team," Ben said.

Hud looked out onto the court. "My dad wants me to transfer there. He says the coaches are better."

"Where do you go now?" Logan asked.

"I'm a freshman at Garfield."

Ben could hardly contain his excitement. "You should definitely transfer! We could use a point guard like you."

"How can you transfer?" Logan asked.

"I just have to say I want to study something at Roosevelt that they don't have at Garfield."

"Like what?"

"My dad says they teach Chinese at Roosevelt," Hud said with a shrug. He looked up at the clock on the gym wall. "I got to go," he added, popping to his feet. "See you around."

"See you at Roosevelt...maybe," Ben called after him as Hud disappeared behind the gym door.

Ben and Logan looked at each other without saying a word. They couldn't believe their good luck.

They had found their point guard.

Chapter 2

"No, no, no!" Ms. Rackey shouted from the podium of the Roosevelt High School music room.

Sitting in the front row of the jazz band, Ben lowered his tenor saxophone as the song slowly died out. He glanced back at Logan, who was standing in the percussion section, and rolled his eyes. The school's music teacher was hard to please.

"You have to play together and listen while you play," she said. She turned toward Ben's section. "The saxophones are playing too fast. Listen to the rhythm. Ellington wants the band to swing—not race—through this song."

The twenty musicians in the Roosevelt "B" jazz band shifted nervously in their metal chairs. Ms. Rackey tapped her baton on the podium. "Let's try it again. Duke Ellington's 'Take the A Train.' One...two...ah, one, two, three, four."

The band started the song again. "That's it. Trumpets a little softer," Ms. Rackey said, raising her voice over the music. "Saxes swing with the rhythm...Hold that note a little longer, Ben. Work the finish."

As he played, Ben could hear the old jazz tune coming to life. He could almost feel the train in the song rumbling uptown under the streets of New York City.

When the band finished, Ms. Rackey smiled. "Better, much better," she called out. "That's it for today, people. Remember, we'll have tryouts for the two soloists next week."

The musicians gathered up their instruments, cases, and sheet music as the music teacher kept talking. "Practice that Gerry Mulligan piece, everyone. The winter concert is only four weeks away. We have to know both pieces by then."

Ben and Logan walked out of the music room and into the crowded, noisy corridor.

"Are you going to try out for a solo?" Logan asked.

"No way. I'm not good enough," Ben answered. "And you know she'll pick Adam Kinner and Tina Termini anyway. They can really play." He swung his saxophone case around to avoid a collision with an oncoming student. "I just like being part of the band."

"Yeah, it's cool," Logan agreed. "Like that last song, when everyone was playing together." He started to tap out the rhythm of "Take the A Train" against his geometry book.

"Hey, have you seen Hud at all?" Ben asked as they walked.

"I think I saw him come out of the assistant principal's office on Monday," Logan said.

"Really?"

"Yeah. It looked like he was with his dad. They were shaking hands with Mr. Clarke outside his office."

"Remember, Hud said his dad wanted him to transfer for hoops?" Ben said, his voice filling with excitement.

"Yeah, but I haven't seen him around yet," Logan said.

"I wonder if he signed up for the basketball tryouts," Ben said. "Let's stop by the gym and check the bulletin board before math."

The boys threaded their way through the halls. Ben kept shifting his saxophone from side to side to make sure he didn't clunk anyone with the case. Soon they stood outside the office of Mr. George, the school's gym teacher and freshman basketball coach. Two large sheets of paper were tacked to the bulletin board. Ben and Logan read the notice announcing the team tryouts.

RHS FRESHMAN BOYS BASKETBALL TEAM TRYOUTS

- Tryouts for the freshman boys basketball team will be conducted Tues., Nov. 15th–Fri., Nov. 18th from 3-5 p.m.
- Open to any freshman boy with at least a 2.0 grade point average.
- The 14-game season begins Dec. 6th.
- At least 12 players will be selected.
- Sign up on the sheet next to this announcement— please print neatly!
- Students who do not sign up before 3 p.m. on Tues., Nov. 15th will not be allowed to try out.

Stop by my office if you have any questions. Hope to see you at the tryouts!

HEAD COACH: Mr. George
ASSISTANT COACHES: Mr. Hukill
Mr. McCracken

Then they scanned the list of kids who had signed up.

"What's Hud's real name?" Logan asked.

"Don't know," Ben said, his eyes still moving down the second sheet.

"There's Andrew, Jordan, and Alan," Logan said.

"We've got our forwards." Ben smiled. "And there's Levon. He's going to pass out in shock when he sees Hud play."

"You mean, *if* he sees Hud play," Logan said. "I don't see him on the list."

Ben pressed closer to the bulletin board.

Kier Palmer-Klein
Kenny Drew
ANTONIO HUDSON
Peter Gonzalez
Eugene Wright

"There he is!" Ben said. "Antonio Hudson. See?"

"You sure that's him?"

"Of course, I'm sure," Ben said, smiling. "That's got to be Hud."

He stepped back from the list and smiled. "We're going to have a great team."

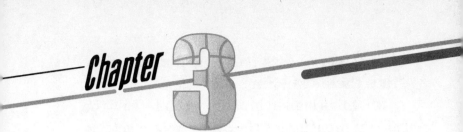

Chapter 3

Ben and Logan hopped off the L7 bus and jogged through the Saturday morning sunshine to the Westwood Recreation Center.

"I wonder if there will be a different crowd on the weekend," Logan said as they turned the corner.

"Maybe," Ben said.

As the boys got closer, they saw that all the outside courts were packed. The sounds of the games—players shouting, shoes scraping against pavement, balls hitting backboards—rose into the early November morning.

"I hope Hud's here," Logan said.

"He seems like the kind of guy who's

always here." Ben spied a familiar face. "Hey, there's Mr. Sims. Let's go ask him."

Mr. Sims smiled broadly when he saw the boys approaching. "Hey, you two are getting to be real regulars around here."

"Hi, Mr. Sims. Is Hud inside?" Ben asked.

"Nobody's inside," Mr. Sims said with a quick shake of his head. "They're painting the gym. It's closed until Monday." He looked around at the busy courts. "We got lucky. It's a beautiful day to play hoops outdoors."

"So is Hud around?" Ben asked.

"Oh, sure," Mr. Sims answered, sounding surprised by the question. "He's on the court in back. That's where the best players are." He started walking away. "Come on, I'll show you where they are. I want to check out the games anyway."

Ben, Logan, and Mr. Sims made their way to the back of the building, zigzagging through the players standing around waiting to play.

"Did Hud transfer to Roosevelt?" Mr. Sims asked.

"Yeah." Ben nodded.

"So when are those freshman team try-outs?"

"Tuesday," Ben answered.

"Is Mr. George still the freshman coach up there?"

"Yeah."

"He's a good coach," Mr. Sims said. Then he cast a stern eye at Ben and Logan. "Be sure to listen to him. He knows his hoops. He'll get you guys ready for varsity." Then Mr. Sims suddenly stopped walking. "Is Hud trying out?"

"Yeah," Ben said. "He's signed up."

Mr. Sims thought for a moment. "The kid plays a little wild, but...." His voice trailed off and he pointed at the back court. "There he is."

The three of them walked over and stood at the side, studying the action.

"There sure are a lot of older guys in this game," Ben said. "Hud's the youngest guy out there by far."

"This is the regular Saturday morning crowd," Mr. Sims said. He began pointing

out some of the players. "There's Fitz...
Joe...Helicopter. And see the chunky guy
over there in the black sweats—the one
with the ball?"

"Yeah." Ben watched as the player spun
around, flipped up a quick jump shot that
swished through the net, and jogged
upcourt, shouting, "You can't stop that shot!
You can't stop that shot!"

"They call him Donut," Mr. Sims said.

Ben grinned. "Why?"

"He eats 'em all the time and now he's
kind of shaped like one." Mr. Sims chuckled
and added, "But believe me, he can shoot
the ball."

A player standing nearby looked over at
Mr. Sims. "Remember that summer league
game? The one when Donut poured in fifty
points against that hotshot college kid?" He
snapped his fingers. "What was his name?
Played for Lafayette."

"Billy Evans," Mr. Sims said. "He *gradu-
ated* from Lafayette. He played some pro
ball in Europe later."

"Man, but Donut owned him that night.

He couldn't miss," the player went on, getting more and more excited with the memory. "Donut might have scored *sixty* that night."

"That's just summer ball," Mr. Sims said with a wave of his hand.

"It's still hoops," the player protested.

"Not real hoops," Mr. Sims insisted. "Guys don't play defense as hard. Heck, some of the guys don't even show up for every game of summer ball. It's not like playing for a high school team or college team. On those teams, you have to show up. Your teammates are depending on you. "

On the court, Donut tossed a two-handed pass up toward the rim. Another player rose high above the crowd, caught the ball with two hands, and jammed it through the basket.

"Whoa, did you see that?" Logan said.

"Watch out for the rim, Helicopter!" Mr. Sims shouted. "I don't want you breaking it."

Laughing, Donut turned to the players on the side. "That's game. Who's got next?"

Hud walked off the court, looking disappointed with his team's loss. Five new players hustled onto it and started shooting around, greeting the other players with handshakes and fist bumps.

"Okay, let's run," Donut said. And the game started.

Hud spotted Ben and Logan and his face brightened. "Hey, guys. I got next game. You want to play?"

"With those guys?" Logan said, nodding toward Donut and his team.

"Why not?" Hud answered. "We can beat them."

"Sure, we'll play," Ben said.

"What?" Logan said.

Mr. Sims nudged Hud. "Pick up the guy over there with the real long arms. They call him 44-Long. He can cover Donut. And Derrick, the guy next to him, is okay."

On the court, Donut's team made quick work of their opponents. They scored on long jump shots and fast-break baskets.

"They look pretty good," Ben whispered to Mr. Sims.

"Anybody can look good if nobody plays defense. Just cover them tight and run them. They'll get tired."

Donut tossed in a final basket and called out, "Who's got next?"

Ben, Logan, Hud, 44-Long, and Derrick headed onto the court.

"Look at this—school must be out," Donut teased, looking at Ben, Logan, and Hud. "We got the young guys playing the old guys. Think you can beat the veterans? Okay, let's go."

Donut's team hit some early jump shots and grabbed a quick 3–1 lead. But Logan snatched a rebound and tossed a pass to Hud. In a flash, Hud raced downcourt, faked left, then bounced a perfect pass to Ben, who scored with an easy layup.

A steal by Hud and another easy layup tied the score, 3–3. Hud's basket sparked the team. Ben hustled to get open and Hud fired passes straight to him for open jump shots. Ben made them all.

"Who's got that guy?" Donut shouted in frustration. "He can shoot." He dribbled slowly upcourt. "What's the score?"

"9–6," Hud said. "We're up. Game to ten."

"Okay, playtime for the kiddies is over," Donut said. "Time to get serious." He spun to his left and leaned back for a jump shot. But 44-Long was all over him and the ball bounced off the rim.

Hud grabbed the long rebound and dribbled downcourt with Ben trailing the play. Suddenly, Hud flipped a behind-the-back pass to Ben at the foul line for a wide-open jumper. The ball bounced up off the loose metal rim, then touched the backboard and found the bottom of the bucket!

"We won. Kids rule!" Hud shouted as Ben, Logan, and the rest of their team traded high-fives.

Mr. Sims stood on the sidelines, nodding with approval. "You guys will do just fine at tryouts."

Chapter 4

Tweeeeet! A whistle shrieked in the Roosevelt High gymnasium. Thirty freshman hopefuls stopped shooting at the six baskets around the gym, and a strange silence settled over everyone.

"Let's line up over here." Coach George pointed to the padded wall under the far basket, then began to pace in front of the players. The coach was average height with close-cropped hair. He wore dark blue gym shorts and a white T-shirt that said "Roosevelt Basketball."

"He looks like he can still play," Logan whispered to Ben.

"Yeah," Ben said. "I heard he was a point guard in college." He elbowed Hud on the other side of him. "You better listen to this guy."

"Let's find out who's who here," Mr. George said, looking at his clipboard. "Hold your hand up and say 'here' when I call your name."

He made his way down the list. "Antonio Hudson," he said, finally coming to Hud's name.

"Here," Hud said. He raised his hand as high as his shoulder.

"Put your hand way up," Coach George ordered. "So I can see it." He continued down the list until the final name was called. "Anyone whose name I didn't call?" he asked. Silence. "Good," the coach said, and handed the clipboard to one of his assistants.

"We have thirty players trying out," Coach George said, starting to pace again. "I only have twelve team uniforms. So this is a competitive situation." He paused, pivoted, and continued. "There will be four days of tryouts. The freshman team is designed to prepare you to become varsity players. Roosevelt High School has had twenty-one consecutive

winning seasons and we've won eight confer-
ence championships." He pointed at the con-
ference championship banners hanging on
the far wall. "At the end of the week, the
players who hustle, play hard, and show me
they are willing to be coached will have a
chance to be part of that tradition."

Ben stood in line, staring at the banners.
He couldn't wait to get started.

"Any questions?" Coach George asked.

Silence again.

"Okay, let's go."

The coach did not take it easy on the first
day of tryouts. He put the players through
their paces.

Dribbling drills.

Baseline-to-baseline sprints.

Tests to measure jumping skills and
quickness.

Coach George and his assistants, Mr.
Hukill and Mr. McCracken, kept moving
around the floor, giving instructions, asking
names, and taking notes.

After an hour of drills and still another
sprint, Ben, Logan, and Hud leaned against

the wall, gasping for air.

"Are we ever going to shoot the ball?" Ben said, catching his breath.

Logan wiped the sweat from his face. "I guess he wants to see who's really in shape."

"Maybe," Hud said. "But you can't tell who can play until you let them play." He straightened up and put his hands on his hips. "What are you guys complaining about, anyway? Coach already knows you. You'll make the team, easy."

Just then, Coach George blew his whistle. "All right, line up!" he shouted, pointing to the same wall. "This time by height."

The boys lined up. Logan—the tallest in the group—stood at the far end. Ben took a place toward the middle. Hud, who was shorter, stood a few places down from Ben.

"All right now, count off by fives," Coach George ordered.

The boys counted off.

"One...two...three...four...five... One... two..."

Both Ben and Hud called out the number four. They traded glances, knowing they would be on the same team.

Quickly, the coaches organized games on the two cross-courts, shuttling in a new team every five minutes. Mr. Hukill and Mr. McCracken refereed the games while Coach George kept an eye on both games and took notes.

Hud started fast, driving past a defender and scoring on a twisting layup. Then, on defense, he tipped a pass, scrambled for the ball, and got it. Balancing on one foot, he fired a long pass to Ben, streaking down-court. Ben looked up just in time, caught the ball, and laid it up and in.

The next time down, Hud drove to the basket and tossed a pass to Ben for an open fifteen-foot jump shot.

Swish.

"Good shot, Ben," Coach George called. "All right, let's switch it up. Ben's team stay out there. Let's hustle."

Five new players came onto the court, but no one on the new team could stop Hud either. He weaved in and out of the defense, sending passes to teammates who turned them into easy shots.

Ben hustled to get open, and whenever

27

he did, Hud would work his magic and suddenly the ball would appear in Ben's hands.

After two easy wins, Ben and Hud sat on the sidelines, drinking water with their backs against the cool, hard cinder block wall. They traded fist bumps.

"Good shooting," Hud said. "Those games at Westwood must be paying off. You're a cinch to make the team."

"What about you?" Ben replied. "Nobody can cover you."

Hud shrugged. "These games are easy. I'm used to Westwood, where some guy like Donut is always fouling me."

Coach George walked down the sidelines, glancing at his notes and giving advice to the players. When he got to Ben and Hud, the boys stood up.

"Nice shooting, Ben." The coach smiled. "I saw you play last year and your shot looks even better now. Remember to keep your elbow in when you shoot, and follow through."

Coach George eyed Hud and checked his notes. "Antonio Hudson, right?"

"Yeah," Hud said. "Everyone calls me Hud."

"Nice job running the offense and getting Ben the ball," the coach said. "Try to keep your dribble lower. And make the simple pass. None of that fancy French pastry."

"French pastry?" Hud asked.

"Fancy passes," the coach explained. "Where do you play?"

"Westwood."

"How's Mr. Sims these days?"

"Good." Hud smiled.

"Tell him Coach George said hello."

Ben elbowed Hud after Coach George moved on. "Sounds like he likes your game."

"I'm not so sure," Hud said. "What was that stuff about French pastry?"

"Forget that," Ben said, shrugging. "He knows who you are. That's important. He's just telling you what you have to do to get better. I'm telling you, you're in."

"Maybe." Hud didn't sound convinced. "When do we find out?"

"Friday."

"How's he going to tell us?"

"He'll just post the team online, on the Roosevelt website."

Coach George blew his whistle. "Okay, let's switch it up. Hudson, get your team out there."

Ben grinned at Hud as they jogged out to the court. "*Your* team?" he said. "You're definitely in. We're going to be playing some real hoops together this season."

Chapter 5

Ben stared out the window of the L7 bus as it wound its way through the rain-slicked streets on Saturday morning, edging closer and closer to the Center.

"Let me see the list again," Logan said.

Ben pulled out his phone and punched in the school's website. The two boys studied the list of names for the twentieth time.

RHS FRESHMAN BOYS BASKETBALL

The following players should report to practice on Nov. 21st at 3:30 p.m.

Andrew Milstein	Logan Moore
Jordan Ferraro	Sam Molina
Levon Efford	Marcus Belanger
Alan Dawson	Antonio Hudson
Ben Williams	Evan Fuller
Anthony Bellino	Brooks Lebow

HEAD COACH: Mr. George
ASSISTANT COACHES: Mr. Hukill
Mr. McCracken

"I told Hud he'd make it," Ben said.

"No kidding," Logan said. "He's the best ball handler and passer on the team by far."

Ben sat back and pressed his knees against the plastic seat in front of him. "You at center, me at shooting guard," he said, almost daydreaming. "Hud at point guard. Andrew and Jordan at forward. We're going to have a great team."

"Eighth and Westwood," the driver called.

Ben and Logan tumbled off the bus and jogged to the Center. The morning was cold and gray, with the unmistakable feel of winter coming.

When they arrived, only a few younger kids were playing on the outdoor courts.

"I guess everyone else is inside," Logan said.

"Yeah. Let's find Hud. I want to make sure he knows he made it." Ben opened the main door of the Center and waved to Mr. Sims, who was on the phone behind the desk. The director waved back.

The gym was packed. And it was loud. Both courts were buzzing with action, with players taking quick shots, calling to each other, and trash talking. The bleachers were filled with other players waiting for their chance to play.

Ben spied Hud standing in a corner, dribbling a basketball between his legs.

"Hey, Hud!" Ben called as he and Logan approached. Hud looked up and stopped dribbling. "You made the team!" Ben said.

Hud spun the ball on his fingertip. "Yeah, I heard."

"We got the roster." Ben held up his phone. The three boys sat down on the bleachers and studied the list on Ben's phone.

"That kid Jordan can play," Hud said.

"But I don't think Anthony should've made it," Logan said. "He can't shoot."

"He's okay," Ben said. "He just didn't do very well during tryouts."

"Where's Tyson?" Hud asked. "I thought he was pretty good."

"What team are you guys talking about?" Donut asked. He was sitting a few feet down the bench.

"The Roosevelt freshman team," Logan said.

"Is Coach George still coaching?" Donut asked.

Before Ben could answer, another player from two rows up interrupted. "George ain't a good coach," he said.

"What do you know?" Donut frowned.

"I played for him."

Donut leaned back and laughed. "Yeah, you played for him. For about five minutes. He threw your lazy butt off the team because you didn't play any defense."

"He was messing with my game," the player insisted. "Never let us run. Always slowing it down—"

"And making you play defense," Donut broke in.

Ben looked at Donut. "Did you ever play for Coach George?"

"I never played high school ball," Donut said. "But I could have," he added quickly. "I was a lot better than those guys on the team. Guess I just didn't want to." He put his hands in back of his head. "I ruled in summer ball. You can ask anybody around here, they'll tell you: Donut ruled summer ball."

He grinned at Ben, Logan, and Hud. "I got next, you want to run?"

He didn't have to ask twice. They all jumped up.

Donut looked back at the player who had complained about Coach George. "Hey, Hi-Tops, we need a fifth player. You want to run too?"

"Sure."

"You gonna play some defense?"

"Give it a break," Hi-Tops said.

Donut's team owned the court. Hud handled the ball and ran the offense. Logan and Hi-Tops took care of the rebounding. Ben and Donut shot the eyes out of the basket, hitting jump shot after jump shot.

"Hi-Tops doesn't play any defense at all," Logan complained under his breath to Ben and Hud between games.

"Neither does Donut," Ben said.

"Yeah, but at least he can shoot," Hud pointed out.

The team won four games in a row. They finally lost when Donut got tired and his shots started to bounce off the rim.

"Man, I couldn't *buy* a basket that last

game." Donut sighed as the team sat down on the bleachers. Ben took a place at the end of the bench, close to where Mr. Sims stood along the wall, watching the games.

"You boys had a good team," Mr. Sims said. "You could have kept the court all day if you'd played some more defense."

Donut looked at the clock on the gym wall. "I got to get to work," he announced. He grabbed a basketball and headed out of the gym.

Hud stood up. "I'll go see if I can find a couple guys who want to play with us."

Ben turned and looked up at Mr. Sims, who was still leaning against the wall. "Donut said he never played high school ball," he said. "I can't believe that. He can really shoot."

Mr. Sims stared off into the distance. "You're right, I don't think he ever did play hoops in high school," he said.

"Donut also said he was better than most of the guys who played on the team," Ben said. "I can believe that."

"Well, it's easy to *say* you're better. It's a

little harder to prove it." Mr. Sims smiled. "But don't get me wrong. Donut's a good guy. He coaches a team of fifth graders here at the Center."

"Really?" Ben said.

"Yep." Mr. Sims nodded. "Believe me, all of his kids can shoot."

"Hey, Ben! Logan! I got us in a game over here," Hud called, waving his arms from the other side of the gym. Ben and Logan popped off the bench to join him.

As Ben waited in the middle of the noisy, crowded floor for the game to start, he glanced back over his shoulder at Mr. Sims. The director was still leaning against the far wall, studying the players. But his mind seemed far away, as if he was remembering something from a long time ago.

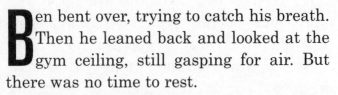

Chapter 6

Ben bent over, trying to catch his breath. Then he leaned back and looked at the gym ceiling, still gasping for air. But there was no time to rest.

"Next three over here!" Coach George shouted. "Let's do it right."

Ben lined up with Hud and Logan. Ben's light gray T-shirt was dark against his wet skin.

"Go!" Coach George called.

Ben, Logan, and Hud took off, weaving their way down the court, trading lanes non-stop as they sent rapid-fire passes to each other. Coach George kept up a steady stream of instructions as the boys sprinted forward. "Come on, I don't want to see the ball touch the floor. Two-handed chest passes. Right on the numbers, every time. No fancy stuff—just good, solid passes. All right, next three…"

After Ben, Logan, and Hud finished the drill, they leaned against the gym wall.

"This guy never lets up," Logan said.

"Are we ever going to scrimmage?" Hud asked.

"Yeah, we've barely shot the ball," Ben said. "Just run, run, run."

Tweeeeet!

All the players and basketballs stopped.

"Okay, let's have three lanes and three basketballs now. We're going to practice full-court defense. The coach stepped out in front of the team to demonstrate. "Get your rear end down," he said, slapping his own backside and getting into a defensive stance. "Hands to the side, move your feet. Stay low. Don't cross your feet." Coach George scurried across the gym like a crab, keeping his hands at his side and staying low. "Okay, Ben, Andrew, and Levon, you're on defense. And let's have three dribblers."

Three other players stepped forward.

"Okay, pair up with Ben, Andrew, or Levon. Try to dribble past them but stay in your lane. Let's go!"

Ben got down into his defensive stance. He shifted from side to side, trying to stay in front of his dribbler. But it was hard to please Coach George.

"Come on, move those feet. Don't reach with your hands!" he shouted. "Stay low, Ben. Shooters have to play defense too."

Ben could feel his thighs burning as he darted across the floor, trying to stay low and constantly pressing the dribbler. When he reached the end of his lane, the next dribbler stepped up to challenge him.

It was Hud.

Oh no, Ben thought as the first dribbler passed the ball on to Hud. *This is gonna be really tough.*

Right away, Hud got past Ben with a quick crossover dribble. "Come on, Ben!" Coach George shouted. "Get in front of him. Beat him to the spot."

Hud kept slipping by Ben with ease, but

Coach George found fault with him, too. "Keep your dribble low, Hudson. No high-stepping. Low dribble. All right, next three on defense."

Ben jogged back to the bench for his water bottle, pulling his sweat-soaked shirt away from his skin. "Coach George is brutal," he whispered to Logan.

"Yeah. Now I see why Donut and those Westwood guys never played for him. I don't think he's ever going to let us scrimmage."

Sure enough, Coach George kept up a steady stream of basketball drills.

Passing.

Rebounding.

More defense drills.

And worst of all, loose-ball drills. In those, Coach George rolled a ball out between two players and both of them had to dive toward it headlong, their elbows and knees scraping and skidding across the polished floor.

After almost two hours of nonstop running and drills, Coach George blew his whistle.

"Finally," Ben said. "He's going to let us scrimmage."

"Don't bet on it," Hud said, pointing to the clock. "It's almost five."

Coach George nodded toward the stands. "Everybody sit down. I have a couple things to give you before I let you go today."

The players grabbed seats in the wooden bleachers. "Told you," Hud said to Ben in a low voice. "No scrimmage."

Coach George stood with his whistle dangling from a thin rope around his neck. In his basketball shorts and crisp, white T-shirt, he looked cool and relaxed.

"Good work out there," he said. "We'll scrimmage next practice, but I wanted to go through those drills first."

All the players groaned and Coach George smiled. "I'm sure you guys all thought you were in good condition," he said. "Well, there's a big difference between being in good condition and being in *basketball* condition."

Still sweating and breathing heavily on the bench, Ben was beginning to understand what the coach was talking about.

"Ben Williams," the coach said.

Startled, Ben looked up.

"You're going to be my captain this season."

"Captain?" Logan whispered. "Do we all have to salute you now?"

"I expect my captain to be a leader on the floor and to tell me if there is anything going on with the team that I should know about." Coach George nodded to his assistant, who began handing out two pieces of paper to each player. "Mr. Hukill is passing out the game schedule for the season."

Ben eagerly studied the list.

RHS FRESHMAN BASKETBALL SCHEDULE
ALL GAMES ARE AT 3:30 PM

Date	Opponent
Tuesday 12/6	Putnam Valley HS
Friday 12/9	@ Kennedy HS
Tuesday 12/13	Hornell HS
Friday 12/16	@ Frostburg HS
Tuesday 12/20	Robinson HS
Friday 12/23	Wilson HS
	>>>>Winter Break<<<<

Friday 1/6	@ Marshall HS
Tuesday 1/10	@ Lewistown HS
Friday 1/13	Austin Prep
Tuesday 1/17	Centerville HS
Tuesday 1/24	@ South Frostburg HS
Friday 1/27	Woods Academy
Saturday 1/28	Adams Prep Tournament
Sunday 1/29	Adams Prep Tournament
Friday 2/4	@ Wyngate HS
Friday 2/11	@ Kilby HS

HEAD COACH: Mr. George
ASSISTANT COACHES: Mr. Hukill
Mr. McCracken

"I know you guys are interested in the games," the coach went on, "but the second handout is even more important. That's where you'll find the rules for playing on my team. If you break any of these rules, you will be suspended from the team. I'm telling you this now so there are no misunderstandings later."

Ben looked at the second sheet.

ROOSEVELT HIGH SCHOOL BASKETBALL

Playing basketball for Roosevelt High School is a privilege, NOT a right. Breaking any of the following rules may lead to a player's suspension from the team. The duration of the player's suspension will be determined solely by Coach George.

Team Rules:
1. Be on time for all team practices and games
2. "On time" for games means dressed and ready 30 minutes before game time
3. If a player must be late for practice or a game, he is required to inform the coach immediately
4. Players should be in bed every night no later than 11 p.m.
5. Players should be in bed on the night before a game no later than 10 p.m.
6. Players must maintain at least a 2.0 grade point average (GPA) throughout the season
7. Players should not argue with coaches, referees or game officials
8. During the season, players should not play "pickup" basketball or games at the play ground or recreation centers
9. Players are permitted to practice dribbling or shooting on their own.

HEAD COACH: Mr. George
ASSISTANT COACHES: Mr. Hukill
Mr. McCracken

"Read them over closely," Coach George said. "Pay special attention to Rule Number Eight: No pickup basketball. I don't want anyone getting hurt or developing any bad habits by playing pickup hoops. But don't worry. You'll get plenty of basketball playing for me."

Ben leaned back toward Hud, who was sitting behind him. "Guess we can't play at Westwood anymore."

Hud didn't answer.

"Any questions?" Coach George asked. He looked around. "Good. Then I'll see you all tomorrow at three. Be ready to run." The coach walked toward his office as the boys headed toward the locker room.

"When's our first game again?" Logan asked.

Ben looked back at the schedule. "A week from Friday, against Putnam Valley."

"How are they?"

"They're usually pretty good," Ben said. "They'll probably be tough."

"They'll be easy," Hud said as he opened the door to the locker room.

"Why do you say that?" Ben asked.

Hud shrugged. "Compared to one of Coach George's practices, *anything* should be easy."

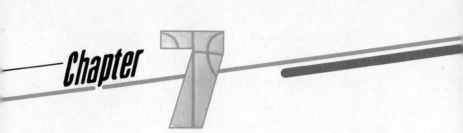

Chapter 7

Listen up!" Coach George called over the noise in the Roosevelt gym. The freshman team huddled around him in their silky, dark blue Raiders uniforms. Ben bounced up and down on the balls of his feet. He could hardly wait to get started.

It was the Raiders' first game of the season. They were playing the Putnam Valley Tigers. Parents and students from both teams sat in clusters in the stands. Two referees waited for the teams at the center of the floor.

"Okay, here's the starting lineup," Coach George said.

Ben caught Logan's eye. They had been

looking forward to this moment for weeks. They'd figured they'd be starting at shooting guard and center, but they were both wondering whether the coach would tap Hud or Levon as starting point guard. At times, Hud played spectacularly in practices, amazing everyone with his behind-the-back dribbling and no-look passes. But Coach George was always after him for turnovers and for taking too many chances on defense.

"Logan will start at center," Coach George said, checking his clipboard. "Andrew and Jordan will play forwards. Ben, you're at shooting guard. And Levon will be at point guard."

Ben and Logan traded glances, then looked over at Hud. Their friend was staring straight ahead, but he seemed okay with the news.

"We're going to begin the game with our half-court, man-to-man defense," Coach George said. "Remember, take care of the ball on offense. Good, solid passes. I don't want to see a lot of turnovers."

Both teams seemed nervous as the game began. They didn't try any fast breaks. Instead, they played slowly, as if they were afraid of making mistakes. Levon set up a couple of early baskets by Logan, but the Tigers stormed back and pulled ahead, 8–4.

A few minutes into the game, Hud and another Raider bounced off the bench to replace Levon and Andrew. Right away, the Raiders offense popped into high gear and started running. Hud dribbled downcourt, charging full speed to the basket. At the last moment, he flipped a pass to Ben, who was wide open at the three-point line. Ben sent up a long jump shot. *Swish!*

The next time down, Hud found Ben again with a no-look pass for another jumper.

Swish!

Roosevelt had grabbed the lead, 9–8!

They still held the lead, 17–14, when Coach George gave Ben and Logan a breather.

"I don't know why Coach didn't start Hud at point guard," Ben whispered to Logan as they sat on the bench. "We do a lot better with him in there."

Logan took a big gulp of water. "Yeah, and you're better when Hud plays. He seems to find you no matter where you are."

"Just like at Westwood." Ben smiled, thinking about his open jump shots.

On the court, Hud threaded a low bounce pass through a maze of players. But the ball bounced out of bounds.

"Green ball." The referee signaled in the direction of the Tigers basket.

Coach George stomped his foot. "Make the simple pass, Hudson. Simple pass! No French pastry!"

He turned and marched down the bench. "Levon, go in for Hudson," he ordered. Levon jumped up and jogged to the scorer's table. Ben and Logan didn't say a word to each other.

The score was tied 23–23 as Coach George gathered everyone together before the second half. "Keep playing man-to-man defense," he said. "On offense, move the ball around for a good shot." Then he seemed to look right at Hud. "Remember, make the easy pass. No fancy stuff."

Coach George checked his clipboard. "Okay. Same starters: Logan, Andrew, Jordan, Ben, Levon... Let's go."

The Roosevelt offense sputtered at the beginning of the second half and the team fell behind, 30–25. Ben was relieved when he looked over and saw Hud kneeling at the scorer's table, waiting to come in.

But Hud's first no-look pass surprised Ben and bounced out of bounds.

"Simple passes!" Coach George shouted again, but this time he left Hud in the game.

It was a good decision. On defense, Hud reached out and tapped a crosscourt pass loose. He grabbed the ball just before it bounced out of bounds, then leaped and fired a perfect overhead pass to Ben, who sprinted downcourt for an easy basket.

Logan rebounded a missed shot and tossed a quick pass to Hud, who took off, dribbling furiously. He outran two defenders, spun, and found Ben set up at his favorite spot—on the left wing, just behind the three-point arc. Hud shot the ball right to him.

Ben wasted no time and sent the ball flying toward the hoop.

Swish! The score was tied, 30–30.

The game went back and forth, with the teams trading baskets. Coach George shuttled players in and out, substituting for Ben, Logan, and Hud. But as the clock ticked down to the final minutes, all three were in the game.

With less than a minute to go, the Tigers sent up a shot. The ball bounced around the rim and fell away. The two teams battled wildly for the ball. A Tiger grabbed it.

Another shot.

Another miss.

This time, Logan soared above the crowd to snap down the rebound. He passed the ball to Hud, who dribbled calmly downcourt.

Ben quickly checked the scoreboard as he ran toward the basket.

VISITOR   RAIDERS
42   0:20 QTR 42
            4

The game was tied, 42–42, with just twenty seconds to play. Coach George stood at the bench, holding up one finger. "One last shot!"

Everyone in the bleachers was standing up and shouting. Hud kept control of the ball, constantly checking his teammates' positions.

I've got to get open, Ben thought. He was closely guarded, so he faked right and sprinted left, running the defender into Logan and getting open for just a split second. Hud spotted him and slipped a pinpoint pass through a tangle of hands and bodies.

Ben grabbed the pass. *Not much time*, he thought. *I have to shoot…quick.* He spun and squared his shoulders to the basket.

Eyeing the front rim, he let go a smooth jump shot.

Swish! The Raiders were ahead!

The Tigers tried desperately to inbound the ball. But the buzzer sounded before they could get a shot.

The Roosevelt Raiders had won, 44–42! As the team swarmed off the bench, Ben looked across the court at Hud. Hud pointed at him and mouthed the words, "Nice shot."

It was almost like being at Westwood.

Chapter 8

One...two...three...four," Ms. Rackey counted off. The Roosevelt jazz band started the winter concert with "Jeru," the Gerry Mulligan tune. Sitting with the saxophones, Ben concentrated on the sheet music and tried to play the song the way he had practiced it so many times. *Here comes the tricky part*, he thought as his fingers slid up and down the keypads.

After his part of the song was finished, Ben relaxed and laid his sax across his lap. He listened as Adam and Tina played their solos, letting his mind wander from music to basketball.

So far, the season was going great. After their close opening win, the Raiders had won the next three games easily. Coach George still complained about Hud's "fancy French pastry" passes and played Levon more often, but at least the team was winning. Of course, Coach didn't seem to mind during the last game when Hud had hit Logan with a cool, behind-the-back pass for an easy layup.

Ms. Rackey lifted her baton and the last notes of Adam's tenor sax echoed through the auditorium. Ben picked up his own instrument again and joined the rest of the band for the last part of the song.

The band was doing great. Logan and the rest of the percussion section had set the rhythm, and the bass plucked out the beat. Even the horns were all playing together. *The band is a pretty good team too*, Ben thought.

Loud applause washed over the band as the song finished. Adam and Tina took a bow. Then everyone filed offstage to make room for the Roosevelt chorus.

Later, sitting in the back of his family's car with his instrument case, Ben could still hear the music in his head.

"That was wonderful, Ben," his father said as he got behind the wheel. "You kids did a terrific job."

"Adam and Tina were fantastic," Ben's mother added. "You'll have to tell them that at school tomorrow."

"I don't think you'll have school tomorrow, if you ask me," Mr. Williams said, shaking his head. "It smells like it's going to snow."

"Smells like snow?" Ben asked.

"When you grow up in New England like I did, you can always smell a snowstorm coming. And I'm telling you, it's going to snow tonight." He pointed to the windshield. Sure enough, a few snowflakes were already hitting the glass. "What did I tell you?"

Ben's phone beeped, telling him he had a text.

"Who's texting you?" his mother asked.

"Logan," Ben said, checking the message. "If we don't have school tomorrow he wants to go sledding at the golf course."

"Well, get some sleep tonight, just in case

you do have school," his mother told him. "Remember, when you were little, you used to sleep with your pajamas on inside-out to get a snow day?"

"Yeah," Ben said, embarrassed.

"You won't have to," Mr. Williams said. "Look." The snow was swirling now in the night air, dancing in the car's headlights.

"Hey, isn't that the Westwood Rec Center, where you guys play basketball?" Ben's father asked.

Ben looked out the window. "Yeah, but we can't play there during the season. Coach won't let us."

"Do you mind if we stop?" Mr. Williams asked. "I'd like to see the place."

"It's getting late," Ben's mom said. "It's after nine o'clock."

"It'll just take a minute."

After Mr. Williams parked the car near the Center, he and Ben hurried toward the building with their heads down against the falling snow. They stepped though the doors and brushed the snow from their hair and jackets. Inside, there was no one behind the desk. The rec center seemed strangely quiet and empty.

Ben could hear noises from the gym. He went over to the Plexiglas window to check out the action.

"Sounds like a game," his father said, coming up behind him.

"Yeah, look," Ben said. The gym was empty except for ten players battling for the ball in a fast-paced game.

Ben's eyes locked on a player in red shorts, dribbling upcourt. The kid pushed a perfect one-hand bounce pass to another player, who cut to the basket for an uncontested layup.

Ben couldn't take his eyes off the passer. *He looks like Hud,* Ben said to himself. Sure enough, when the kid jogged back on defense, Ben saw that it was definitely him.

Mr. Williams turned to Ben. "That's one of your teammates, isn't it? I thought you said..."

Ben turned away from the window. He didn't want Hud to notice him. "Come on, Dad. You've seen the place. Let's get going, okay?" He moved quickly past the front desk to the doors.

His mind was racing. What was he going to do? Hud was definitely breaking the team rules by playing at Westwood. *I'm the captain,* Ben thought. *Should I tell the coach? Or should I just talk to Hud myself?*

Ben stepped outside and saw more snow swirling in the dark. The sidewalk was already slippery.

"I guess your New England nose must have been right," Mrs. Williams said as Ben and his father settled into the car.

Ben sat back without a word. He hoped it would snow all night so school—and practice—would be canceled tomorrow. He needed more time to think about what he was going to do about Hud.

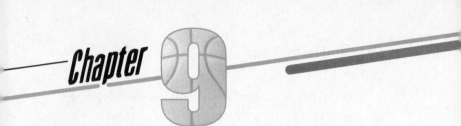

en and Logan pulled their toboggan through the fresh snow blanketing the rolling hills of the golf course.

"Are you sure it was Hud?" Logan asked.

"I told you, I'm a hundred percent sure," Ben answered. "He was playing full court with Donut, Hi-Tops, Helicopter...all the guys."

"By the way, where are we headed?" Logan asked.

"To the twelfth hole." Ben said, looking into the distance. "You know, where that steep hill is."

"What about the hill on the ninth hole?"

"That's for little kids," Ben said.

Both boys knew the golf course well from caddying there during the summer. Now it looked a lot different. The ground was white, and bare tree limbs reached up to the clear December sky. There were no golfers, no carts, and no birds. Just the sound of snow crunching beneath their boots.

"Was Mr. Sims at the Center?" Logan asked.

Ben shook his head. "Nope."

"Do you think he knows Hud is playing when he's not supposed to?"

"Maybe." Ben shrugged. "He usually knows everything that's going on at Westwood."

A strong wind whipped some loose snow into the air. The boys ducked their chins into the collars of their jackets. "Do you think Mr. Sims would tell Coach George about Hud?" Ben asked.

"He might," Logan said. "But he might not."

The pale winter sun ducked behind a cloud. Ben felt a sudden chill.

"It doesn't matter whether Mr. Sims

knows, anyway," Ben said finally. "*We* know. And I've got to decide what to do about it."

"It would really mess things up if Coach suspended Hud," Logan said. "I mean, we're undefeated and Hud is our best passer."

"Yeah, but Hud can't just break the rules and do his own thing. Coach said, 'No pickup games,' and he's going to be really mad if he finds out that Hud's been playing at Westwood."

"Yeah, I guess it's kind of like jazz band," Logan said.

"What do you mean?"

"Well, we've all got to play together or it doesn't work."

"Yeah," Ben said. "You can't have one person running off and playing a different song or something."

The boys walked in silence, dragging the toboggan up the hill near the twelfth hole. Ben pointed to the section of woods at the very top. "There's a cool path in there. That's where we'll start. When we come down the path, it'll shoot us out onto this hill. It's awesome!"

"Have you done this before?" Logan asked, sounding nervous.

"Yeah, last winter, when we had that big storm," Ben said. "You scared?"

"No. I just don't want to get killed."

Ben laughed. "At least then we wouldn't have to figure out what to do about Hud."

"What do you mean *we*?" Logan said, grinning. "You're the captain, remember?"

"Yeah." Ben sighed. "Don't worry. I remember."

They pulled the toboggan up the path and through the woods, until the trees and bushes got too thick to go any farther. Logan turned and looked back down the path to the clearing and the steep hill below.

"Uh, are you sure you've done this before?"

"Yeah," Ben said, He slapped his friend on the back of his jacket. "Don't worry, it'll be great."

They swung the toboggan around so it pointed straight down the path.

"I'll sit in back," Logan offered quickly.

"You *are* scared!"

"Hey, you know the way," Logan said. "And anyway, I'm heavier. We'll need more weight in back."

"Okay," Ben agreed, climbing into the sled. "Give it a good push."

They started down the path, slowly at first, then faster and faster. Ben gripped the front of the toboggan, aiming for the opening at the end of the tunnel of trees. The bushes along the side whipped by as they sailed toward the top of the steep hill.

"Yes!" Ben shouted as they burst out of the woods and into the open. Suddenly, they were flying through the air. Then Logan's weight tipped the toboggan backward as it dropped onto the hill.

Thwack!

The edge of the toboggan caught an icy patch and started to fishtail wildly, spilling the boys across the snow. They tumbled down the hill as the toboggan flew past them.

"Whoa!" Logan shouted, jumping up and shaking the snow out of his jacket. "That was amazing!"

"I told you," Ben said as he got to his feet. "Did you see how high we were?"

"Ten feet in the air, at least," Logan said breathlessly.

They slapped a high-five with their gloved hands. Ben grabbed the toboggan rope. "Want to do it again?"

"Nah," Logan said. "Let's go try the ninth hole."

"I thought you liked this one."

"I did. I don't want to push our luck, that's all." Logan grinned. "And anyway, you've got to talk to Hud, and you can't do that if you kill yourself on the toboggan."

Ben sighed. "I guess I do have to say something, huh?"

Logan nodded. "Yeah, you do. *Captain.*"

"Fine. I'll talk to him tomorrow," Ben said. "After practice."

Chapter 10

Ben spun and shot a fadeaway jumper. The ball swished through the net and he hustled back on defense.

"Okay, tie score, 8–8," Coach George called out. "Remember, it's ten baskets to win. The losers run wind sprints."

"Come on!" Ben shouted to his teammates. "Let's beat these guys." He couldn't believe Roosevelt's first stringers were having so much trouble beating the second stringers. *If we had Hud instead of Levon at point guard, we'd be killing them*, he thought.

Hud brought the ball downcourt. He faked right and, with a quick crossover, drove past Levon to the basket. Then he tried to slip a wraparound pass to Sam, the second-string center. But the ball bounced through Sam's hands, off Logan's leg, and out of bounds.

"Yellow ball," Coach George said, pointing in the second team's direction. "Hudson, make sure the person's ready for the pass!"

As the scrimmage resumed, Hud tried to dribble by Levon again. But this time, Ben stepped in to stop him. Thinking quickly, Hud flicked a pass to Marcus Belanger, the second team's shooting guard, for an open jumper.

Swish!

"Yellow team leads, 9–8," Coach George said.

"Come on, we need a good shot," Ben told his teammates as they ran up the floor.

But Hud surprised everyone. Instead of running to play defense upcourt, he spun quickly and played tight defense against Levon in the backcourt, forcing him to stop his dribble.

"Help!" Levon called, desperately shifting the ball from side to side as Hud waved his arms all around him.

Ben darted back toward Levon, but Hud got a hand on the ball before Levon could make a pass. The ball bounced along the open floor and all three players scrambled after it.

Hud was the quickest. He grabbed the ball, leaped up with a half-twist, and tossed it to Marcus, who laid the ball into the basket for the winning score.

Coach George blew his whistle. Loud. "All right, Logan, Jordan, Andrew, Ben, and Levon. Give me five wind sprints. I want everything you got. Make sure you touch the walls at each end of the gym."

Ben walked to the back of the gym with Logan.

"How did we lose to those guys?" Logan asked, shaking his head.

"Easy," Ben said. "Hud."

Logan looked around and lowered his voice. "Did you talk to him about Westwood?"

Ben shook his head. "Not yet. I figured I'd talk to him after practice." He stopped as he reached the back wall. "And practice isn't over yet. At least, not for us."

Coach George blew his whistle again and the five tired Roosevelt first stringers began their sprints.

Minutes later, Ben and Logan walked down the stairs to the locker room, towels draped around their necks. Ben could hear the hiss of showers from inside.

Hud stepped out of the locker room just as Ben and Logan reached the bottom of the steps. His hair was still wet from his shower.

"Hey, what's the hurry?" Logan asked him in a teasing voice. "I thought you'd want to hang around and trash talk us about losing to you guys."

"Nah, I just got to go someplace," Hud said.

"Westwood?" Ben asked.

Hud just looked at him, seeming a bit surprised.

Logan reached for the locker room door. "I'll see you guys later. I've got to shower."

Ben eyed Hud. "So *are* you going to the rec center?"

"Maybe later." Hud shrugged. "My dad makes me do my homework first."

"I saw you playing there the other night, you know."

"What? Were you spying on me or something?" Hud sounded annoyed.

"No, my parents and I were just coming home from the winter concert and my dad wanted to see the Center."

Hud took a few steps away, looking like he wanted to take off.

"You're not supposed to be playing pickup games, remember?" Ben said. "It's against the team rules."

"Yeah, I know," Hud said, staring right at Ben. "But I like playing at Westwood." He nodded toward the stairs that led to the gym. "It's a lot more fun than all the drills and stuff Coach George makes us do. Playing at the Center is more like real hoops."

"Coach George is a good coach," Ben said. "Even Mr. Sims said so."

"If he's such a good coach, how come he's starting Levon instead of me at point guard?"

Ben didn't have a good answer for that one. "Hey, we're undefeated," he said finally. "And Coach George plays you a lot. You're just not a starter."

"Well, if he keeps starting Levon, we won't stay undefeated for long," Hud said with a smirk. "We might lose to Robinson tomorrow. They're supposed to be pretty tough."

Ben could feel the salt from his sweat making his skin itch. "If Coach catches you playing pickup, he'll suspend you."

"He won't find out," Hud said. "Who's going to tell him?"

"I don't know," Ben said. "But I'm supposed to. I'm the captain."

"Do what you want." Hud shrugged. "I guess Levon will have to get you the ball in all your favorite spots, then." He started to push past Ben. "I gotta go."

Ben grabbed Hud by the arm. "Listen, you've got to stop playing pickup."

Hud shook free. "I *like* playing at Westwood, okay?" he snapped. "It makes me a better player."

"Yeah, but—" Ben started.

"And that will help the team," Hud broke in. "More than Coach's stupid rules."

He pushed open the door and let it slam behind him.

A gust of cold air blew in and Ben just stood there for a long time. Finally, he turned slowly and headed into the locker room, feeling like he had just lost the biggest game of the season.

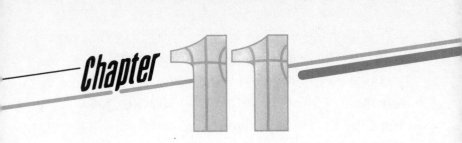
imple pass, Hudson!" Coach George shouted from the bench after yet another turnover. "Simple pass!"

Ben checked the scoreboard as he ran back on defense.

VISITOR 39   2:15   QTR 3   RAIDERS 33

The Roosevelt Raiders trailed the Robinson Panthers by six points in the third quarter. Ben looked over at the Raiders bench. Coach George stood with his arms folded, as if he was thinking of his next move.

I hope he keeps Hud in, Ben thought.

Logan ripped down a missed shot and whipped a pass to Hud, who quickly took the ball up the middle of the court as Ben raced along the right. At half-court, Hud zipped a no-look pass to the right, but Ben was a half step behind. The ball bounced off his fingertips and out of bounds.

Coach George slapped the bench and signaled to Levon to get ready. The next time the referee blew his whistle, Levon went in for Hud.

I should have caught that pass, Ben thought. *Then Hud would still be in the game.*

"Be careful, Levon!" Coach George shouted after him. "Remember, you already have four fouls."

Hud dropped down on the end of the bench and leaned back. He wiped his face with a towel and threw it on the floor in frustration. "Come on, Raiders!" he called. "Let's come back."

Slowly, the Raiders started to inch back into the game. With Levon running the offense and getting the ball to Logan on the inside and Ben on the outside for open jump shots, the Raiders pulled within two points of the Panthers. With three minutes to go in the game, the score was 47–45. The Raiders were pumped. They could win this one!

"Come on, Raiders."

"We need a stop."

"Good defense, good defense."

The Panthers point guard brought the ball downcourt and they started passing it around, looking for a good shot. Ben saw a chance for a steal and bolted toward the action. He almost intercepted a pass, but the ball slipped past his fingertips.

"Help!" Ben shouted as the Panther he was supposed to be guarding drove to the basket.

Levon stepped into the player's path just as he tossed up a shot. Levon and the Panther collided and tumbled to the floor.

Tweeeeeeeet!

The referee blew his whistle and pointed at Levon. "Blocking foul on Number Fifteen!"

"Sorry," Ben said as he reached down and pulled Levon up.

The horn sounded. The official at the scorer's table held up five fingers. "That's five fouls on Number Fifteen."

Hud reported to the scorer's table and went into the game for Levon. Coach George shouted instructions from the sideline. "Simple passes. No French pastry. Just run the offense."

The fouled Panther player stepped to the line and calmly hit two free throws. The Raiders trailed by four with two minutes to go, 49–45.

The teams traded baskets and Roosevelt still trailed by four. One minute to go. Hud took a chance on defense, darting out and tipping the ball away from the Panthers dribbler.

A pack of players dove for the loose ball. Ben and a Panther player both wrapped their arms around the ball. The referee blew his whistle and looked at the scorer's table. The possession arrow pointed to the Roosevelt bench.

Ben pumped his fist as the team cheered.

"All right!"

"Comeback time!"

"Need a basket!"

In the Raiders' next possession, Ben curled around a clump of players as Hud dribbled near the foul line. Hud quickly spotted Ben and slipped a pass right off his dribble, getting the ball by the Panthers defense and into Ben's hands. Ben tossed up a quick shot that rattled around the rim and dropped in. He glanced at the scoreboard as he raced back on defense.

Two down with 25 seconds to go, Ben thought. "Tough D!" he shouted, getting down into his defensive stance.

The Panthers passed the ball around as precious seconds ticked off the clock.

"Foul him, foul him!" Coach George screamed, waving his arms and jumping off the bench. Ben grabbed the player with the ball.

"Time out." Coach George signaled after the referee called the foul on Ben. He gathered the team around him on the sidelines. "Okay, we've got one time out left and they're shooting one-and-one," the coach said. "If he misses his first shot, get the ball, get it over half-court, and call time out. Then we can set up a play and get a good shot. Let's go."

The Panthers player at the foul line took a deep breath, bent his knees, and sent a shot spinning toward the hoop. "Short!" he shouted. The ball clanked off the front rim.

Logan got the rebound and tossed a pass to Ben, who dribbled quickly downcourt. "Time out!" he shouted the moment his feet passed the half-court line.

Back on the sidelines, the Raiders formed a tight circle around Coach George as he diagrammed the final play on his clipboard.

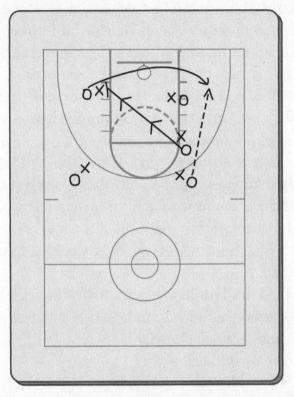

"Hud will look for Ben with a two-point shot," he said, pointing at the play. "Take the shot as soon as you can, Ben. Logan, Andrew, and everybody else hit the boards, just in case he misses."

Ben felt his heart pump faster as he walked back onto the court. He lined up exactly where he was supposed to and ran the play just as Coach George had directed. But when he looked back for the pass from Hud, it wasn't there. Hud looked at Ben, but instead of passing, he dribbled to his left, beyond the three-point line—and launched a long jump shot.

That's not the play, Ben thought. He raced toward the basket, desperately hoping for a rebound. Then he watched the ball float through the air, almost in slow motion.

"No!" Coach George bellowed from the bench.

The ball didn't even touch the rim. It splashed though the net, barely moving the strings. A perfect swish!

"Yes!" Ben cried.

The Roosevelt Raiders mobbed Hud in the middle of the court. Logan pulled Ben out of the circle as the rest of the team jumped up and down together. "Now Coach has *got* to start Hud," he said.

Chapter 12

Ben glanced at the clock on the gym wall: 4:40. *Only twenty minutes left of practice,* he thought. *Is Coach ever going to let us scrimmage?*

Coach George had not been happy with the Robinson game, even though the Raiders had won. So he was drilling them extra-hard during practice.

Layup drills.

Passing drills.

Rebounding drills.

But this time they were even more grueling than ever.

Logan leaned against the wall to catch his breath. "Guess we're not going to scrimmage," he said to Ben.

"Guess not," Ben said. He was watching Hud cover Levon in a one-on-one defense drill. Coach George was right on top of Hud, shouting instructions. "Come on, Hudson. Keep your legs moving. Get your rear end down. Move your feet, don't reach with your hands."

Ben leaned toward Logan. "Just think what practice would have been like if Hud had *missed* that last shot."

Tweeeet!

Coach George blew his whistle. The whole team looked up, still hoping for a scrimmage. "Fast-break drill," Coach George snapped. He pointed around the gym. "Give me three lines. I want good, crisp chest-passes. Right on the numbers. I don't want to see that ball touch the floor."

Ben spied Hud across the gym. His friend caught his eye and shook his head.

The Roosevelt players weaved back and forth across the gym, running and passing at top speed. Luckily, the ball never touched the floor.

Tweeeeet!

Coach George blew his whistle again. Ben checked the clock: 4:50.

"All right, we've still got ten minutes," the coach announced. "Let's have a quick scrimmage. He grabbed a handful of bright yellow mesh jerseys out of a bag and began tossing them to the starters.

Logan...

Jordan...

Andrew...

Ben...

Coach George paused for a second, then tossed the final yellow shirt to Levon.

Ben glanced at Hud again. His jaw was clenched and his eyes were blazing.

"Hey, Coach," Logan said, "when are you going to let Hud run with us?"

"When he learns how to run the plays the way I plan them," Coach George answered without a hint of a smile. "Listen up, all of you. We have to run the plays the way I draw them up in the huddle. That gives us the best chance to win." He stood with the ball on his hip and looked from player to player until his eyes settled on Hud. "We got lucky last game with Hudson's shot. But we don't want to be lucky. We want to be good."

He scooped the ball to Hud. "Okay, Hudson, your team's ball."

Hud played as if he was angry at the whole world and had something to prove. He dribbled furiously downcourt, fast-breaking past Levon to the basket, pulling up for jump shots, and passing to teammates from every possible angle.

But this time the first-string team was determined not to lose. They kept the score tied with baskets by Ben and Logan.

"One minute to go," Coach George announced. "Next basket wins."

Hud dribbled to the right, trying to get by Levon. But Levon played tough defense and cut off his path to the basket. Sensing that Hud was going to try to win the game all by himself, Ben left his man and snuck up behind him. Hud suddenly reversed direction and ran up against Ben, who knocked the ball loose. Ben scrambled after the ball, with Hud trailing and pulling at him.

Ben finally grabbed the ball near the sideline and looked upcourt. He tossed a pass to Levon, who was wide open. Levon laid the ball into the basket.

"That's game," Coach George called. "We don't have time for the losers to run wind sprints now. They'll run next practice."

Ben saw that Hud was already moving toward the locker room even though the coach was still talking. "See you tomorrow at three o'clock sharp. We're playing Wilson. They're undefeated, too, so be ready to play your best."

"Good game," Logan told Ben as they walked across the gym. "We needed every one of your baskets."

"Yeah. I really thought Hud was going to beat us again," Ben replied. "All by himself."

"He sure left fast," Logan said. "Do you think he was mad or something?"

"Don't know." Ben shrugged.

The two boys walked into the locker room as Hud was heading out. He had thrown his winter jacket on over his practice uniform and he was still sweaty. The gym bag slung over his shoulder was half open and his clothes were spilling out.

"Hey, where are you going?" Ben said.

"Yeah, no hard feelings on the loss, right?" Logan teased.

"I'm out of here," Hud said. "I'm not running any wind sprints for that guy."

"What do you mean?" Logan asked.

"Coach is never going to start me." Hud almost spit out the words. "Even after I won that last game for us."

"Hey, Coach is tough on everybody," Ben said. "He's just trying to get us ready for varsity. He's trying to make us all better players."

"No, he isn't!" Hud said. "He's trying to make me play the way *he* thinks I should play. And he's got all those dumb rules." He pushed open the door.

"Wait a minute, where are you going?" Ben asked.

Hud looked back over his shoulder. "To Westwood," he said. "To play some *real* hoops."

The L7 bus was almost empty. Ben sat near the back and fiddled with the handle of his saxophone case as he tried to think of how to convince Hud not to quit the team. He gazed out the window as the bus rumbled downtown. The streetlights cast an eerie glow on the passing sidewalks.

Ben wished he hadn't lied to his parents and told them he was practicing music at Logan's house. But he didn't see any other way. He couldn't tell them he was going to Westwood—at night—to talk to Hud. They would have told him to let Coach George handle it.

But Ben was the Raiders' captain. It was his job to try to talk to Hud...again.

"Eighth and Westwood," the driver announced.

Ben swung his saxophone case around the bus pole and stepped off the bus. He slipped the case over his shoulder and zipped his coat. Then he plunged his hands into his pockets and walked quickly, head down, to the Center.

Inside, the Center was warm. Ben began to sweat. Maybe it was the heat. Or maybe it was because he was nervous. He loosened his jacket and followed the sounds of a basketball game in progress. Looking down through the Plexiglas window, Ben spotted Hud. He was dribbling toward the basket, looking free and happy. Donut, Hi-Tops, and 44-Long were there, too, with a bunch of other players.

For a long time, Ben stood there, watching.

"You're a little late for band practice," said a voice behind him.

Ben turned and saw Mr. Sims. The director nodded toward the saxophone case.

"We, uh, had an extra practice after school tonight," Ben said.

Mr. Sims raised a questioning eyebrow. "What are you *really* doing here on your own, at this hour?"

"I was looking for Hud."

"Well, you found him," Mr. Sims said. "He's here most nights."

"He's not supposed to be," Ben said in a small voice. "It's against the team rules."

Mr. Sims smiled. "I figured that might be the case," he said. "But Coach George runs his team his way. I run Westwood my way. It's tough to stop a kid from playing ball, especially one who loves the game as much as Hud."

Mr. Sims and Ben looked back down at the game, just as Hud pushed out a long bounce pass that skipped ahead of his teammate and out of bounds. "So, what's going on?" Mr. Sims asked.

A sudden wave of sadness swept over Ben. He almost felt like crying. "I think Hud's going to quit the team," he said finally.

"Now why would he want to do a crazy thing like that?"

"I guess Coach wasn't playing Hud as much as Hud thought he should," Ben said. "And he's real tired of all the drills and stuff."

"Mr. George is a good coach. A real good coach," Mr. Sims said. He paused a moment and added with a chuckle, "Of course, he can be pretty stubborn. Sometimes, it's his way or the highway."

"Hud's *got* to come back," Ben blurted out. "The team really needs him."

Mr. Sims nodded. "Yeah, he should probably go back. But maybe not for the reason you think."

"What do you mean?"

Mr. Sims looked at Ben as if he was sizing him up. "You want Hud to play because he's a good passer," he said. "And sure, Hud can get you and Logan the ball where you guys can score—"

"Well, yeah, but—" Ben began.

"You guys want to win," Mr. Sims went on. "Right?"

"Sure," Ben said.

"Nothing wrong with winning." Mr. Sims looked down on the court as Hud hit Donut with a perfect behind-the-back pass. "But I want Hud to be the best player he can be."

Ben didn't say anything. He could tell that Mr. Sims was just warming up.

"You see those guys down there?" Mr. Sims said, pointing to the court. "Donut could shoot the eyes out of the basket when he was your age. But he never played on a school team past eighth grade. And Hi-Tops? He led his high school team in rebounds as a sophomore. Never played again after that."

"Why not?"

"Said he didn't like the coach." Mr. Sims shook his head. "Those two had a chance to get some real coaching—improve their game. Who knows, they might have even had the chance to play ball after high school."

"But Donut and all those guys still played summer ball, right?" Ben said. "And they still play here."

Mr. Sims nodded. "Yeah. But here's the thing: summer ball and playing here are okay for practice, for trying to get better. That's why I let Hud play so much here." He paused. "But pickup shouldn't be the only ball you play. At some point, you need to test yourself in a real game. Roosevelt has coaches, referees...even people who pay money to see the games."

Mr. Sims continued to stare down at the game. "Believe me," he added softly, "the playgrounds and rec centers are full of guys who could have been great." He crossed his arms. "When I lived back in New York City, I played summer ball on the playgrounds with guys folks still talk about."

"Really? Like who?" Ben asked.

"Well, The Goat, for one."

"Who?"

"Earl Manigault," Mr. Sims explained. "They called him 'The Goat.' Man—that guy could jump. He was famous for his 'Double Dunk.' He would leap up, dunk a ball, catch it, and dunk it again before he came back down."

"Cool," Ben said.

"And score?" Mr. Sims went on. "Nobody could stop The Goat. I saw him rack up sixty points one night in the Rucker League."

"What's the Rucker League?"

"That's the big summer league in New York City," Mr. Sims explained. "All the best players played in the Rucker League."

"Did The Goat ever play in college or the pros?" Ben asked.

Mr. Sims shook his head. "That's the thing," he said. "He played with Kareem Abdul Jabbar, Earl 'The Pearl' Monroe, Connie Hawkins, and all the great New York players during the summer."

"Really?"

"Yeah, but he never went up against those guys in the big games when they were playing their hardest. In pickup ball, everyone remembers the dunks and points," Mr. Sims went on. "But they forget the turnovers or the times when the guy you're supposed to be covering scores."

"Coach George is always getting after Hud for turnovers and defense," Ben said.

"That's right. Coaches remember those things."

Ben suddenly had an idea. "Mr. Sims, could *you* talk to Hud?" he asked. "I tried to do it because I'm the team captain, but he wouldn't listen to me. Maybe he'll listen to you. I mean, maybe you could tell him about The Goat, and how he never really tested himself in real games."

Mr. Sims looked down at the game again. Donut hit a jump shot and jogged down-court, talking and laughing. "I'll try, but I don't know how much good it'll do," he said, sounding a little tired. "I've talked to just about every one of those guys down there."

He turned back to Ben. "When's your next game?"

"Tomorrow at home, against Wilson."

"Wilson? They're always tough. I'll talk to him tonight," Mr. Sims said. "But I can't promise you he'll listen." He checked his watch. "You'd better get going, young man. The next L7 is heading back your way in a few minutes. There probably won't be another one for at least an hour."

96

"Thanks, Mr. Sims." Ben grabbed his saxophone case and headed for the bus stop. Maybe, just maybe, Mr. Sims could pull off a big win for the Raiders by convincing Hud to come back.

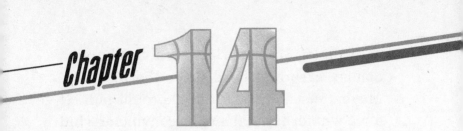

Chapter 14

The red numbers of the clock on the locker room wall changed again.

2:55

Ben pulled the laces of his high-top basketball shoes tighter. "Did you see Hud today?" he asked Logan in a low voice.

"Just between classes, in the hall," his friend answered.

"Did he say anything to you? You know, about staying on the team?"

Logan shook his head. "No," he said. "I'll bet he's on his way to Westwood right now."

Ben sighed. "Coach is going to be here at

three o'clock. And if Hud isn't...." He didn't finish the sentence. He didn't need to.

Just then, Hud burst into the locker room and swung his backpack into a metal locker with a loud bang. He started tearing off his school clothes like they were on fire.

Ben couldn't believe it. Hud was back! "Hey, I didn't think you were going to show up," Ben said. "The game's about to start."

"Hey, I got a couple minutes to spare." Hud grinned as he pulled on his Raiders uniform.

Coach George walked in as Hud was lacing up his basketball shoes. "Listen up, everybody," he said. "Big game today. We've got to play well. Wilson is 5–0, too." He pulled over a large whiteboard from the corner of the room. "We'll start Logan, Jordan, Andrew, Ben, and Levon, but let's push our defense out and try to pick them up closer to the half-court line."

He sketched the new defense plan on the whiteboard as he talked.

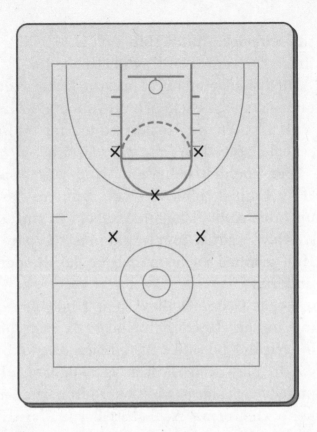

"Let's put some pressure on them. Force Wilson to make some bad passes." Coach looked around the circle of players. "Don't worry about getting tired. I'm going to use lots of substitutions today. Just play hard every minute that you're in the game. Okay, let's go."

The team jogged up the stairs to the gym. Ben fell into step with Hud.

"Glad you made it," he said. "Maybe we can win today."

"Yeah," Hud said. "We better."

During warm-ups, Logan asked Ben, "Hey, do you think Hud is okay?"

"Yeah," Ben said. "He'll be fine."

The Wilson Warriors jumped to a quick lead in the first quarter. The Raiders kept up the defensive pressure and hung close. Coach George kept his promise about shuttling players in and out of the game.

When Hud came in, he wasted no time setting up Ben in his favorite jump-shot spots. Slowly, the Raiders started gaining on Wilson. Then Hud slipped a perfect bounce pass to Logan, who spun to the hoop and laid it in. The Raiders had cut the Warriors' lead to two points, 17–15!

Hud was on top of his game and Coach George stuck with him for most of the second quarter. The teams traded baskets as the Warriors clung to a two-point lead, 29–27.

With a minute to go in the half, Logan snatched a rebound off the glass backboard and snapped a pass to Hud. The ball had barely touched Hud's hands before he flung it to Ben who was sprinting downcourt.

Ben caught the ball in full stride and dribbled to the basket for an easy layup to tie the game. He pointed a finger at Hud as he raced back on defense. "Nice pass," he said as they slapped hands.

"Pressure defense!" Coach George shouted, holding both hands in the air.

Hud snapped into action. Staying low and moving his feet in short, quick steps, he darted in front of the Warriors point guard. The point guard dribbled right into Hud and the two of them collided.

Tweeeeeet!

The referee put his left hand behind his head and pointed at the Warrior player. "Offensive foul," he called. "Charging on Number Twelve."

"Time out!" Coach George called. He grabbed his clipboard as the team, pumped up by Hud's play, gathered around. "Good defense, Hud," he said.

Hud nodded.

Coach George looked at the game clock. Twelve seconds to go in the half and the score was tied. Quickly, he drew up a play on his clipboard.

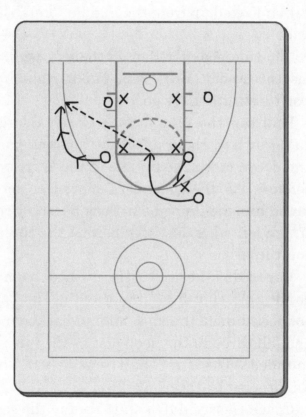

"Let's take a chance and try to get Ben open for a three-pointer. Andrew, get the ball inbound to Hudson." He lifted his marker and pointed it at Hud. "I want you to try to drive down the middle and draw the defense to you. Ben, which wing do you like to shoot from?"

Ben looked up from the huddle. "Left," he said.

"Hudson, look for Ben on the left, behind the three-point line. Ben, put it right up. Don't hesitate. Let's go."

Hud ran the play just as Coach George had drawn it. He grabbed the inbound pass and drove down the middle of the Warriors defense. As the defenders moved to surround him, he flipped a no-look pass to Ben, on the left wing, one step behind the three-point line.

Ben didn't hesitate. He pushed a one-hand jump shot high into the air. The ball bounced up off the rim, hit the backboard, and fell through the hoop just as the buzzer sounded. The first half was over. The Raiders led by three, 32–29!

Coach George didn't start Hud in the second half. But a few minutes later, as soon as

Hud did enter the game, the Roosevelt offense really clicked: passing, fast-breaking, shooting, playing pressure defense. The Raiders' lead grew steadily through the second half. Finally, they were ahead by fifteen points.

People in the stands counted down the final seconds.

"Ten...nine...eight..."

With a sly smile, Hud dribbled down the right side of the court. Sam Molina, Roosevelt's backup center, hustled downcourt on the left.

"...seven...six...five...four..."

Hud zipped a long, behind-the-back pass that hit Sam in stride. Sam laid the ball in the basket just as the buzzer sounded.

The crowd went wild and the Raiders bench was on its feet.

"What a pass!"

"Great look, Hud!"

"All right, Raiders!"

The team was still cheering and smacking high-fives in the locker room when Coach George held his hands up for silence.

The Raiders settled down, a bit slower than usual. "That's the best half of basketball we've played all season," Coach George announced. The locker room filled with cheers again. "And it's a great way to head into the holiday break...undefeated!"

The team took up the chant. "Undefeated...undefeated...undefeated!"

Coach George raised his hands again. "Listen up," he said. "Our next practice will be a week from Monday, after the break. So you guys have a few days off."

More cheers. "But remember," the coach went on, "I still expect you to follow team rules over the break. Except one." He paused and looked around the room. Ben could have sworn he looked at Hud a little bit longer than any of the other players. "If you want to play pickup hoops at Westwood or anyplace else over the holidays, that's okay with me. Just be careful."

Ben and Hud shared a quick fist bump.

"Guess I'll see you tomorrow," Hud said.

"Yeah." Ben grinned. "At Westwood."

Chapter 15

H i, Mr. Sims."

"Good morning, boys," Mr. Sims said, looking up at Ben and Logan from behind his desk. Then his face wrinkled into a question mark. "I thought you boys weren't supposed to play any pickup games?"

"Coach George gave us some time off," Ben explained. "He said it was okay."

"I heard the Raiders played well yesterday," Mr. Sims said.

"We won, 57–40." Ben said proudly. "We're still undefeated, 6–0."

"Hud was amazing," Logan added.

"Yeah," Ben said. "He didn't have any

turnovers and he played great defense." He looked around the Center. "Is he here?"

Mr. Sims laughed. "What do you think?" He motioned behind the desk. "He's down in the gym with all the regulars."

As Ben and Logan headed toward the stairs, Ben looked over his shoulder. "Thanks for talking to Hud, Mr. Sims. Whatever you said really worked."

Mr. Sims chuckled. "Well, I had some help."

"What do you mean?" Ben asked.

Mr. Sims shooed the boys away. "You'd better get in there or you'll miss out on a game. Go on."

The gym was crowded, even for a Saturday morning.

"There he is," Logan said, pointing across the floor.

Hud was leaning against a far wall with Donut and Hi-Tops as they waited their turn.

"Hey, do you guys need a couple players?" Ben asked as he and Logan walked up.

"Yeah," Donut said. "We got the second game after this one."

"That long?"

"Yeah." Donut seemed disgusted. "We lost our first game because Hi-Tops here didn't play any defense. Again."

"What? And you did?" Hi-Tops sounded annoyed. "Quit talking and start hitting some of your shots. We'll be fine."

Donut rolled his eyes and turned back to Ben and Logan. "I hear the Roosevelt Raiders didn't do too bad yesterday."

"We're 6–0," Ben and Logan said together.

Donut elbowed Hud. "I also heard you almost lost one of your star players."

Hud pushed Donut's arm away.

"Yeah," Ben said, looking back at Hud. "But it looks like Mr. Sims talked you into staying."

Hud stared out at the court. "It wasn't Mr. Sims who talked me into staying," he said.

"It wasn't?" Ben asked.

"Oh, he talked to me, all right," Hud said as Donut grinned beside him. "Mr. Sims told me all about that guy, The Goat. And everything he said made sense. But I was still going to quit and just play at Westwood and in the summer league."

"So tell your buddy who made you change your mind." Donut nudged Hud again. Hud elbowed him back, but this time he was smiling.

"Go ahead, tell him," Donut insisted.

Hud pointed with his thumb. "This guy," he said.

"Really?" Ben turned to Donut. "So how come you want Hud playing for Roosevelt now? I thought you just liked summer ball and playing at Westwood."

"I do," Donut said, shrugging. "But, I don't know...I guess maybe I wish I'd played both. Man, if I'd played for Roosevelt, I would have definitely set some records."

"Yeah, for missed shots and not playing defense," Hi-Tops teased.

"That's still not the reason I decided to come back," Hud broke in.

"What was it?" Ben asked.

Hud hesitated.

"Go on, tell your buddy," Donut said.

Hud shrugged. "Donut said I couldn't play for his summer league team if I quit the Raiders."

"You've got a summer league team?" Logan asked Donut.

"Sure, we even got a sponsor," Donut said.

"Who?"

"The Westwood Donut Shop."

"Donut even said he didn't want me playing at Westwood during the season anymore," Hud said, rolling his eyes.

"You can still play both," Donut pointed out. "Pickup in the summer, team hoops for Roosevelt in the winter. Like I should have done."

The game on the nearest court ended and another five players took the court. "We got next," Donut reminded everyone. Then he turned to Ben and Logan. "You guys want to play on my team this summer?"

"For real?" Logan said.

"Sure, why not?" Donut said. "I already got Hud. I could use some more young guys to run the floor, put some pressure on—"

"And play some defense," Hi-Tops added.

Donut shot Hi-Tops an annoyed look. Then he turned back to Ben and Logan again. "What do you say? You could be my Kiddie Squad."

"Okay," Ben said. He grinned at Hud and Logan. "We'll show you old guys how to play some real hoops."

The Real Story

One of the great things about basketball is that it is a simple game. Players don't need much to get a game going besides a hoop, a ball, and a place to play. Although Hud and Donut and the other players at Westwood Recreation Center play five-on-five, full court games, you don't need ten players or even a full court. You can play one-on-one, two-on-two, or three-on-three. Or you can practice dribbling and shooting all by yourself. Players can also play a half-court game using just one basket.

Of course, games played on playgrounds or street courts are a bit different than those played by school teams in gymnasiums or by professional players in the NBA.

Streetball players pick their own teams. Because there are no referees, players call their own fouls. And because there are no coaches, players are often freer to try tricky passes or fancy shots.

One of the most famous basketball playgrounds is Holcombe Rucker Park, also known as "The Rucker," in New York City. The park is named after a city playground director who later became an English teacher in a city school. Holcombe Rucker believed in combining sports with education, and he helped the athletes at his playground with their reading skills and even with their homework.

In 1946, Rucker began the tradition of holding a semi-professional summer tournament in the Harlem section of New York City. The players who either participated in pickup games at the Rucker or played in the Rucker Tournament over the years comprise an All-Star list of the greatest names in basketball. They include:

Kareem Abdul-Jabbar—The leading scorer in the history of the NBA. Abdul-Jabbar attended Power Memorial High School in New York.

Wilt Chamberlain—The only player ever to score 100 points in an NBA game and the leading rebounder in NBA history.

Nate "Tiny" Archibald—The only player to lead the NBA in scoring and assists in the same season.

Bill Bradley—An NBA All-Star and member of two NBA championship teams with the New York Knicks, Bradley was later elected as a United States senator from New Jersey.

Julius "Dr. J" Erving—An eleven-time All-Star from Roosevelt, New York, Erving was known for his amazing jumping and dunking abilities.

The Rucker was also famous for its legendary local players. These players were kings of the playground pickup games but, for one reason or another, never made it big in either college or professional basketball. The players had fancy moves and colorful nicknames such as "Pee-Wee," "The Professor," "Booger," and "Swee' Pea."

But perhaps the most legendary Rucker player was the one Mr. Sims remembered: Earl "The Goat" Manigault.

Manigault was born in Charleston, South Carolina, in 1944, but later moved to Harlem. He loved basketball and practiced the game constantly on the city's street courts, including the one where Holcombe Rucker was the director. Because Manigault practiced with weights on his ankles, he became a legendary leaper. It was said that Manigault could jump and dunk the ball with his left hand, then catch the ball after it had gone through the net and dunk it again with his right hand, all without hanging on the rim.

There are several stories about why Manigault was called "The Goat." According to one story, people often misunderstood when Manigault told them his name. They thought he was saying, "Earl Nanny Goat," and the name stuck. Another story claims that "GOAT" stands for the "Greatest Of All Time."

Even though Manigault played at Rucker

with and against some of the great college and pro players of his day, he never made it as a college or pro player himself. Sadly, Manigault began taking and selling illegal drugs. He even went to prison for robbery because he needed money to support his drug habit.

Later, Manigault quit using drugs and started a basketball tournament in Harlem called "Walk Away From Drugs." He also worked with young people at the city's playgrounds. Manigault died in 1998 at the age of 53.

Basketball players, both older and younger, still play pickup games on playgrounds, street courts, and gyms all over the world. Playing pickup basketball is a great way for any player to improve his or her skills. But it is also important for a player to play and test those skills on an organized team.

John Wooden, the Hall of Fame player and coach whose UCLA teams won a record ten NCAA championships in the 1960s and '70s, once observed that pickup games are not a real test of basketball skills. Wooden said, "Every once in a while I will overhear some young college player talking about beating [NBA superstar] Magic Johnson in a summer pickup game at [UCLA's] Pauley Pavilion. I almost have to bite my tongue to avoid pointing out that the *real* Magic Johnson was not on that floor. The real one stands up in the NBA against a Larry Bird or a Michael Jordan. There is a great difference."

So what kind of basketball should be considered "real hoops"? The pickup games played on playgrounds and street courts, or the more formal games played with referees and coaches on gymnasium floors? Maybe the best answer is the one Ben and Hud found: play both pickup basketball *and* on an organized team with a coach. That way you'll know for sure that you're playing some real hoops!

About the Author

Fred Bowen was a Little Leaguer who loved to read. Now he is the author of many action-packed books of sports fiction. He has also written a weekly sports column for kids in *The Washington Post* since 2000.

For thirteen years, Fred coached kids' baseball and basketball teams. Some of his  stories spring directly from his coaching experience and his sports-happy childhood in Massachusetts.

Fred holds a degree in history from the University of Pennsylvania and a law degree from George Washington University. He was a lawyer for many years before retiring to become a full-time children's author. Bowen has been a guest author at schools and conferences across the country, as well as the Smithsonian Institute in Washington, DC, and The Baseball Hall of Fame.

Fred lives in Silver Spring, Maryland, with his wife Peggy Jackson. Their son is a college baseball coach and their daughter is a college student.

Be sure to check out the author's websites.
www.fredbowen.com
www.SportsStorySeries.com

Become a fan of Fred Bowen on Facebook!

In my research on the Rucker League and Earl "The Goat" Manigault, I consulted the history section of the National Basketball Association's website, *www.nba.com.*

The quote from Coach John Wooden is from his book, THEY CALL ME COACH, written with Jack Tobin.

While TAKE THE A TRAIN, the piece Ben and his school jazz band play for the winter concert, was the theme song of the Duke Ellington Orchestra for years, it was written by Billy Strayhorn.

Finally, the author thanks his daughter, Kerry Margaret Bowen, for her help in typing the original manuscript.

HEY, SPORTS FANS!

Don't miss these action-packed books by Fred Bowen...

T. J.'s Secret Pitch
PB: $5.95 / 978-1-56145-504-1

T. J.'s pitches just don't pack the power they need to strike out the batters, but the story of 1940s baseball hero Rip Sewell and his legendary eephus pitch may help him find a solution.

The Golden Glove
PB: $5.95 / 978-1-56145-505-8

Without his lucky glove, Jamie doesn't believe in his ability to lead his baseball team to victory. How will he learn that faith in oneself is the most important equipment for any game?

The Kid Coach
PB: $5.95 / 978-1-56145-506-5

Scott and his teammates can't find an adult to coach their team, so they must find a leader among themselves.

Playoff Dreams
PB: $5.95 / 978-1-56145-507-2

Brendan is one of the best players in the league, but no matter how hard he tries, he can't make his team win.

Winners Take All
PB: $5.95 / 978-1-56145-512-6

Kyle makes a poor decision to cheat in a big game. Someone discovers the truth and threatens to reveal it. What can Kyle do now?

All-St★r Sports Story
Series

Full Court Fever
PB: $5.95 / 978-1-56145-508-9

The Falcons have the skill but not the height to win their games. Will the full-court zone press be the solution to their problem?

Off the Rim
PB: $5.95 / 978-1-56145-509-6

Hoping to be more than a benchwarmer, Chris learns that defense is just as important as offense.

The Final Cut
PB: $5.95 / 978-1-56145-510-2

Four friends realize that they may not all make the team and that the tryouts are a test—not only of their athletic skills, but also of their friendship.

On the Line
PB: $5.95 / 978-1-56145-511-9

Marcus is the highest scorer and the best rebounder, but he's not so great at free throws—until the school custodian helps him overcome his fear of failure.

Check out **www.SportsStorySeries.com** for more info.